For Eve ~ J.D.

For Princess Amelia ~ L.M.

First published 2006 by Macmillan Children's Books
This revised edition published 2009 by Macmillan Children's Books
a division of Macmillan Publishers Limited
20 New Wharf Road, London N1 9RR
Basingstoke and Oxford
Associated companies throughout the world
www.panmacmillan.com

ISBN: 978-0-330-51384-5

Text copyright © Julia Donaldson 2006
Illustrations copyright © Lydia Monks 2006

The right of Julia Donaldson and Lydia Monks to be identified
as the author and illustrator of this work has been asserted by them
in accordance with the Copyright, Designs and Patents Act 1988.

1 3 5 7 9 8 6 4 2

A CIP catalogue record for this book
is available from the British Library.

Printed in China

Julia Donaldson

The Princess and the Wizard

Illustrated by

Lydia Monks

Macmillan Children's Books

It was Princess Eliza's birthday. She was just blowing out
the seven candles on her cake when a wicked wizard flew down
the chimney and into the room.

"WHY DIDN'T YOU INVITE ME TO YOUR PARTY?"
he thundered.

"Because wicked wizards like
turning people to stone,"
replied Princess Eliza.

"So they do," said the Wizard, and with a flick of his bony fingers he turned the King, the Queen and all the party guests into stone.
Then he laughed a horrible laugh and said to Princess Eliza,
"They like capturing princesses too."

Just then there was a whirring of wings and in through
the window flew the Princess's Fairy Godmother.
She was late for the party.

When she saw what had happened, she waved her wand
and said:

"The Princess may try seven times to escape
By changing her colour and changing her shape."

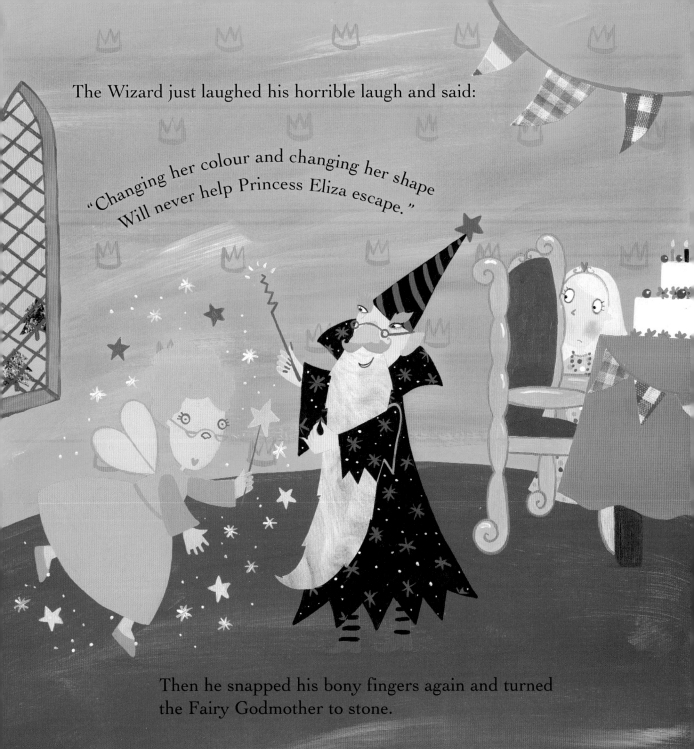

The Wizard just laughed his horrible laugh and said:

"Changing her colour and changing her shape
Will never help Princess Eliza escape."

Then he snapped his bony fingers again and turned
the Fairy Godmother to stone.

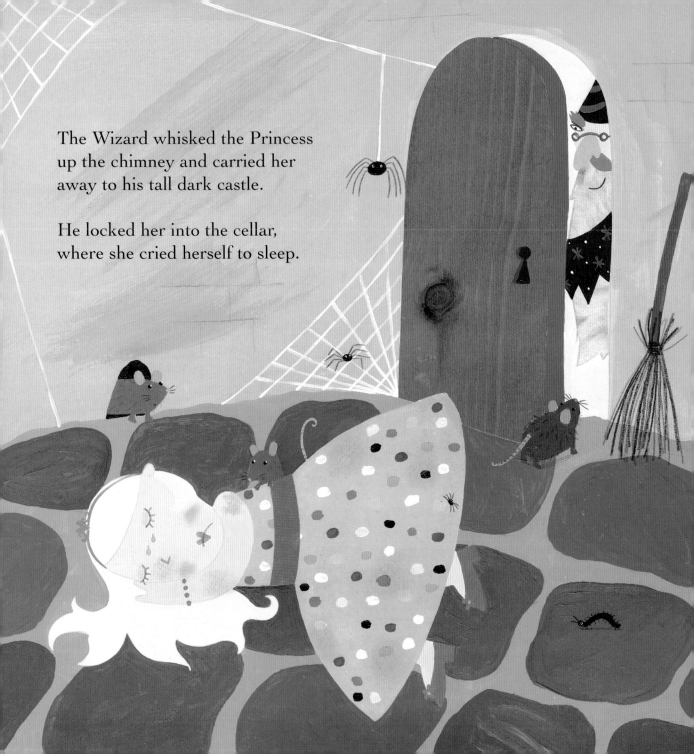

The Wizard whisked the Princess up the chimney and carried her away to his tall dark castle.

He locked her into the cellar, where she cried herself to sleep.

The next day was Monday. The Wizard unlocked the cellar door. He was holding the big fat book which contained all his magic.

"This is your first chance to escape," he said. "I shall count to one hundred and then I shall come and find you."

He opened his book,
closed his eyes and
began to count.

Princess Eliza ran outside.
The moat of the castle shone blue under the blue sky.
She jumped into the water and turned herself into a blue fish.

"Ninety-eight, ninety-nine, a hundred!"
The Wizard opened his eyes, looked in
his magic book and read:

> To find where Eliza
>   is hiding from you,
> Look in the moat
>   for the fish that is blue.

He fished Eliza out of the moat and
took her to his kitchen, which was full
of blue plates and pots and pans. They
were all covered in dried-up food.

"So you like blue, do you?" he said.
"Then set to work and wash!"
And he locked her in.

On Tuesday morning the Wizard unlocked the kitchen door.
He looked at the clean plates and pots and pans and he grunted.

"Chance number two," he said.

Then he opened his book, closed his eyes
and began to count.

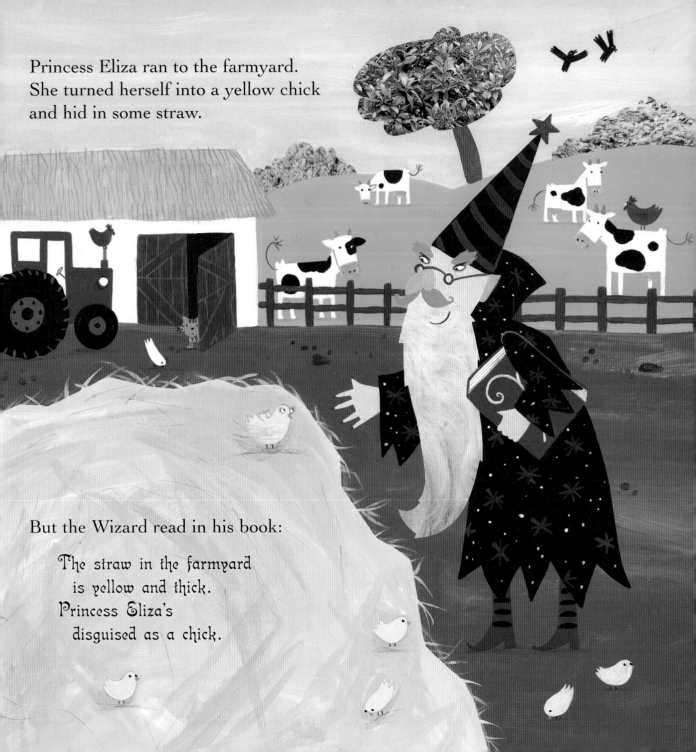

Princess Eliza ran to the farmyard.
She turned herself into a yellow chick
and hid in some straw.

But the Wizard read in his book:

The straw in the farmyard
is yellow and thick.
Princess Eliza's
disguised as a chick.

He scooped Eliza up and took her to a cupboard which was full
of yellow socks. They all had holes in them, made by his pointy toenails.
"So you like yellow, do you?" he said. "Then set to work and darn!"
And he locked her in.

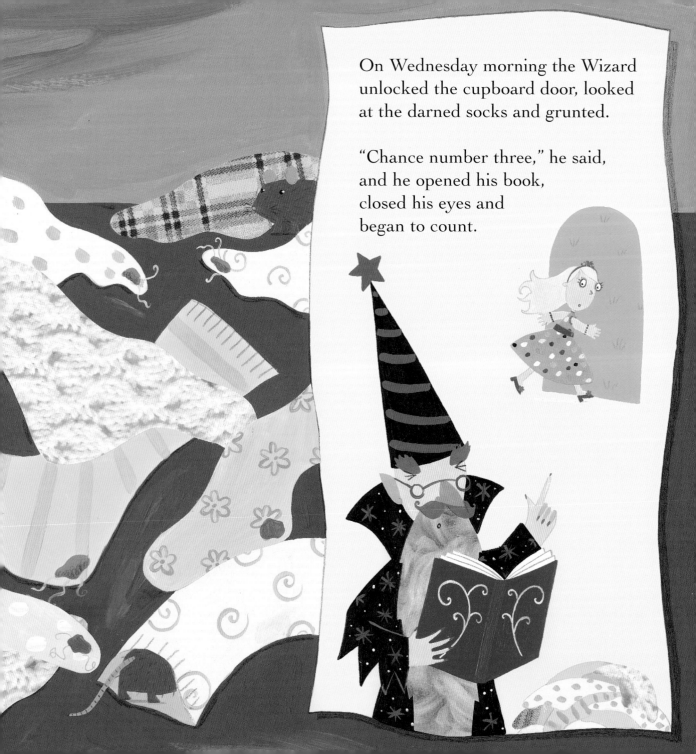

On Wednesday morning the Wizard
unlocked the cupboard door, looked
at the darned socks and grunted.

"Chance number three," he said,
and he opened his book,
closed his eyes and
began to count.

Princess Eliza ran to the meadow.
She changed herself into a green grasshopper
and hid among the grass blades.

But the Wizard read in his book:

The grasshopper princess
      is easily seen
   Chirping away
      in the meadow so green.

He caught Eliza in a net and took her to his green bathroom.
The bath, basin, walls and floor were covered in the Wizard's
slimy toothpaste.

"So you like green, do you?" he said. "Then set to work and wipe!"
And he locked her in.

Three more days went by. Each day the Princess tried to escape.

On Thursday she turned herself into an orange fox and hid in a pile of orange leaves.

On Friday she turned herself into a purple butterfly and fluttered among some purple flowers.

On Saturday she turned
herself into a black cat and
lurked in a black tunnel.

But each time the Wizard found her
and gave her yet more work to do.

On Sunday morning, the Wizard came on to the roof where
Eliza had been scrubbing the sooty chimney pots.
Instead of grunting, he laughed his horrible laugh.

"This is your last chance," he said. "If I catch you this time, you must stay and work for me for the rest of your life."

Then he opened his book, closed his eyes and began to count.

Princess Eliza turned herself into a white gull and flew up into a cloud.

But as she hovered above the roof where the Wizard was still counting, she saw words forming on the page of his open book. "So that's how he finds me!" she cried. "I shall never escape!"

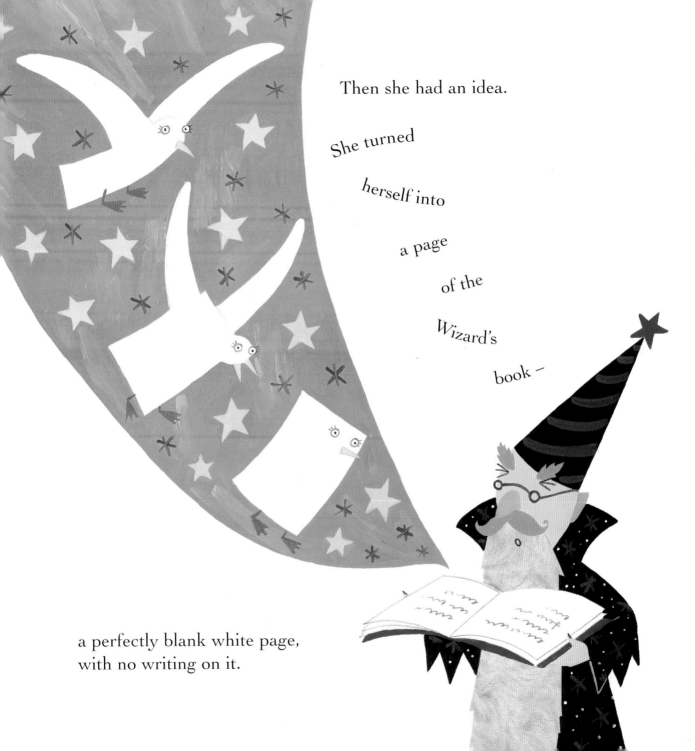

Then she had an idea.

She turned

herself into

a page

of the

Wizard's

book –

a perfectly blank white page,
with no writing on it.

"Ninety-eight, ninety-nine, a hundred!"
The Wizard finished counting and
began to read his book:

> The Princess turned into
> a bird in the sky.
> She hid in a cloud, then
> she had one more try.

That was the end of the page.
The Wizard turned over to read more.
But there was no more. The next page
in his book was blank and white.

He flew into a RAGE!

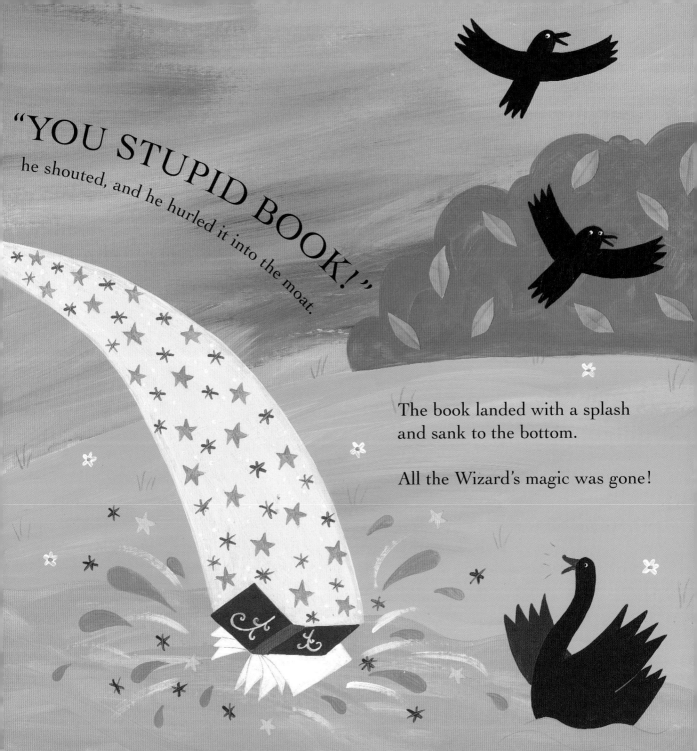

"YOU STUPID BOOK!"
he shouted, and he hurled it into the moat.

The book landed with a splash
and sank to the bottom.

All the Wizard's magic was gone!

At that moment in the palace, the King and Queen
and all the party guests came back to life.

"Where is Princess Eliza?"
they asked each other.

Nobody knew except the Fairy Godmother,
and she only smiled and said nothing.

Princess Eliza had turned herself
from a white page into a blue fish and
was swimming to the edge of the moat.

She turned herself into a
yellow chick and ran across
the corn in the farmyard.

She turned herself into a green
grasshopper and hopped over the grass.

She turned herself into an orange fox and raced through the orange leaves.

She turned herself into a purple butterfly and fluttered over the purple flowers.

She turned herself into a black cat and streaked through the black tunnel.

Then she turned herself into a white bird and flew . . .

. . . all the way back to the palace and in through the window.

She perched on a chair at the tea table
and changed herself . . .

back into a princess!

The King and Queen and all the
party guests hugged her.

Then Princess Eliza cut her birthday
cake and everyone had a slice.